# SOS
# for Rita

*Also by Hilda Offen in Happy Cat Books*

# SOS
# for Rita

*Hilda Offen*

Happy Cat Books

*For Jessica and Laura West*

**HAPPY CAT BOOKS**

Published by Happy Cat Books Ltd.,
Bradfield, Essex CO11 2UT, UK

This edition first published 2004
1 3 5 7 9 10 8 6 4 2

A CIP catalogue record for this book is available from the British Library

ISBN 1 903285 90 9

Printed in China by Midas Printing International Limited

The Potter children were excited. It was the first day of their holiday.

"Can we go to the beach now, Mum?" asked Eddie.

"Yes," called Mrs Potter from inside the caravan. "But take care of Rita – she's only little."

"Oh no!" groaned Eddie, Julie and Jim.

5

They set off down the cliff path, and Rita
trotted along behind.

"Why have you brought that old box?"
asked Jim.

"What a silly thing to bring to the beach," said Julie.

Rita kept quiet. "If only they knew what's inside!" she thought.

They reached the beach and looked along the sands.

"I'm going swimming," said Eddie.

"I'm going for a donkey-ride," said Julie.

"I'm going on the helter-skelter," said Jim.

"You can look after our towels, Rita," they shouted as they ran off.

Rita watched them disappear.

"Oh well, I'll do a spot of sunbathing," she said, sitting down.

She'd hardly closed her eyes when along the beach came the Bertram brothers. Their ball landed on Rita's towel.

"Out of the way, titch!" said Billy.

"Oops! Sorry!" said Boris, pretending to miss the ball, and he kicked sand all over Rita.

"Just you wait!" thought Rita, but she had no time to feel cross.

A scream rang out along the beach. Julie's donkey had bolted and was heading for the rocks!

"This is a job for the Rescuer!" said Rita, grabbing her special box.

"Where can I change?" she wondered. "I
know – the Punch and Judy stall."

In a split second she had put on her
Rescuer outfit. She was ready for action!

"Help!" screamed Julie, clinging on to the donkey's neck.

Rita raced after them like an Olympic sprinter. She grasped the donkey's reins and leaped onto its back.

"Whoa!" she cried, and the donkey skidded to a halt.

"You've saved my little Neddy!" gasped Mr Khan, puffing up behind them.

"And me too!" cried Julie. "Can I have your autograph, please, Rescuer?"

"Another time, perhaps," said Rita, who had spotted more trouble. "I think I'm needed over there."

Mr Muscles, the Strong Man from the
pier, had fallen into the quicksands! And so
had the rest of the Muscles family! They
had been watching a plane doing aerobatics
and had been looking up when they should
have been looking down.

Mr Muscles had sunk up to his chin, Mrs
Muscles up to her armpits, Grandma
Muscles up to her waist, and little Mervin
Muscles up to his knees.

"Help!" they cried.

"Hold on to this!" cried Rita, flying over to them with an oar.

What a good thing Mr Muscles had a strong set of teeth!

"One-two-three-pull!" cried Rita.

Squelch! Slurp! Glug! Pop! – out shot the Muscles family.

"How can we ever repay you?" gasped Mr Muscles, emptying sand from his pockets. But Rita was already zooming off towards the helter-skelter. Jim had been trying to do a headstand on his coconut mat and had shot over the side.

"He'll be killed!" cried the people on the ground.

"Not if I can help it," said Rita, and she flashed through the air at the speed of light.

"Ooh!" gasped the crowd, and "Well-held!" they cried as Rita caught Jim in her arms and set him down safely on the pavement.

"Can't stop!" said Rita.

She had spotted someone else in trouble. Far out on the horizon, a seagull was pecking at Mrs Miller's lilo.

Whoosh! The air rushed out and the lilo started to sink.

"Help!" screamed Mrs Miller.

Rita came skimming over the waves.

"Hang on!" she cried, and she dived into the sea. With three giant puffs she blew the lilo up again. She stuck her finger in the puncture and pushed Mrs Miller back to the beach.

As she stepped ashore, Rita heard someone crying. The Bertram brothers were kicking down Tommy Tiler's sandcastle.

"I've had enough of you!" said Rita. She grasped the bullies by their shirts and whisked them away. Then she hung them from the top of the windsock.

"Help!" screamed Boris and Billy; but no one took any notice.

"That's one rescue I *won't* be doing,"
said Rita, and she helped Tommy build the
biggest sandcastle on the beach.

But Rita's work was not over yet! Out at sea something else was happening. The swimmers splashed around in panic as a dark fin cut through the water.

"Shark!" screamed Eddie, who was directly in its path. "Help!"

"Here I come!" cried Rita, and she seized a coil of rope.

Rita dived down and knotted the rope
round the shark's jaw.

"Now you can't bite anyone," she said.

The shark was furious. It thrashed its tail, it leaped out of the water, it rolled and it dived, but it could not shake Rita off its back. Soon it was completely exhausted.

"Do you promise to go away if I untie you?" asked Rita.

The shark nodded, so Rita untied the knot.

"Off you go!" she said. The shark could hardly wait to make its escape. It would never go near another beach again.

"Hooray for the Rescuer!" cried the
people on the shore. "Hip-hip-hooray!"
They clapped and cheered, and they rushed
forward and gave Rita ice-cream and
candyfloss and lollipops.

"Thank you," said Rita, and ate them
all up.

"Now I need some exercise," she said.

First she headed a beach ball up and down for half an hour. Then she swam ten times between the two piers.

"You can have three thousand free bounces on my Bouncing Castle," said Mr Robinson. "And you can keep your boots on!"

Rita bounced and bounced and bounced until a clock struck seven.

"Time to change!" said Rita, and she slipped back to the Punch and Judy stall.

"Where have you been?" cried Eddie,
when Rita arrived back at the caravan.
"We looked everywhere for you."

"Didn't you see the Rescuer?" asked
Julie.

"She wrestled with a shark!" cried Jim.

"What were you doing?" asked Eddie.

"Oh – just this and that!" said Rita, and
she tucked the box under her bunk.

*Other Rita titles available in Happy Cat Paperbacks*

## Rita in Wonderworld

Abandoned in the Chicks' Nest Play Area, Rita doesn't find Wonderworld much fun. Luckily she has her secret outfit to hand – soon she is tightrope walking, chasing gorillas and rescuing her brothers from a giant spider's web.

## Rita and the Flying Saucer

When a flying saucer lands on earth with a group of aliens from planet Norma Alpha on board it's time for Rita the Rescuer to call on all her special powers. She smashes an asteroid, takes a lost Norm back to the flying saucer and even shows the visitors the quickest way home.

## Roll Up! Roll Up! It's Rita

Rita's family thinks she is too small to dress up for the school fair. But Rita has her own special Rescuer's costume and in the blink of an eye she is saving a hot-air balloon, rounding up sheep and winning the tug-of-war single-handed!

## Arise, Our Rita!

Rita may be the youngest of the Potter family, but she also is the fabulous Rescuer! And teaching archery to Robin Hood, taming dragons and giants, is all in a day's work for our pint-sized superhero.